FRIENDS
OF ACPL

P9-DZA-324

HOLIDAY COLLECTION

Thank You,
THANKSGIVING

For Joyce

Clarion Books
a Houghton Mifflin Company imprint
215 Park Avenue South, New York, NY 10003
Copyright © 2003 by David Milgrim

The illustrations were executed in digital oil pastel.
The text was set in 30-point Blockhead Unplugged.

For information about permission to reproduce selections from this book, write to
Permissions, Houghton Mifflin Company, 215 Park Avenue South, New York, NY 10003.

Manufactured in China

Library of Congress Cataloging-in-Publication Data

Milgrim, David.
Thank you, Thanksgiving / by David Milgrim.
p. cm.
Summary: While on a Thanksgiving Day errand for her mother,
a girl says thank you to all the things around her.
ISBN: 0-618-27466-9 (alk. paper)
[1. Thanksgiving Day—Fiction.] I. Title.
PZ7.M59485 Th 2003
[E]—dc21
2002013365

SCP 10 9 8 7 6 5 4 3 2 1

Thank You,
THANKSGIVING

by David Milgrim

Clarion Books

New York

Thank you for
sending me, Mom.

Thank you, warm boots.

Thank you, pretty clouds.

Thank you, rabbits.

Thank you, park.

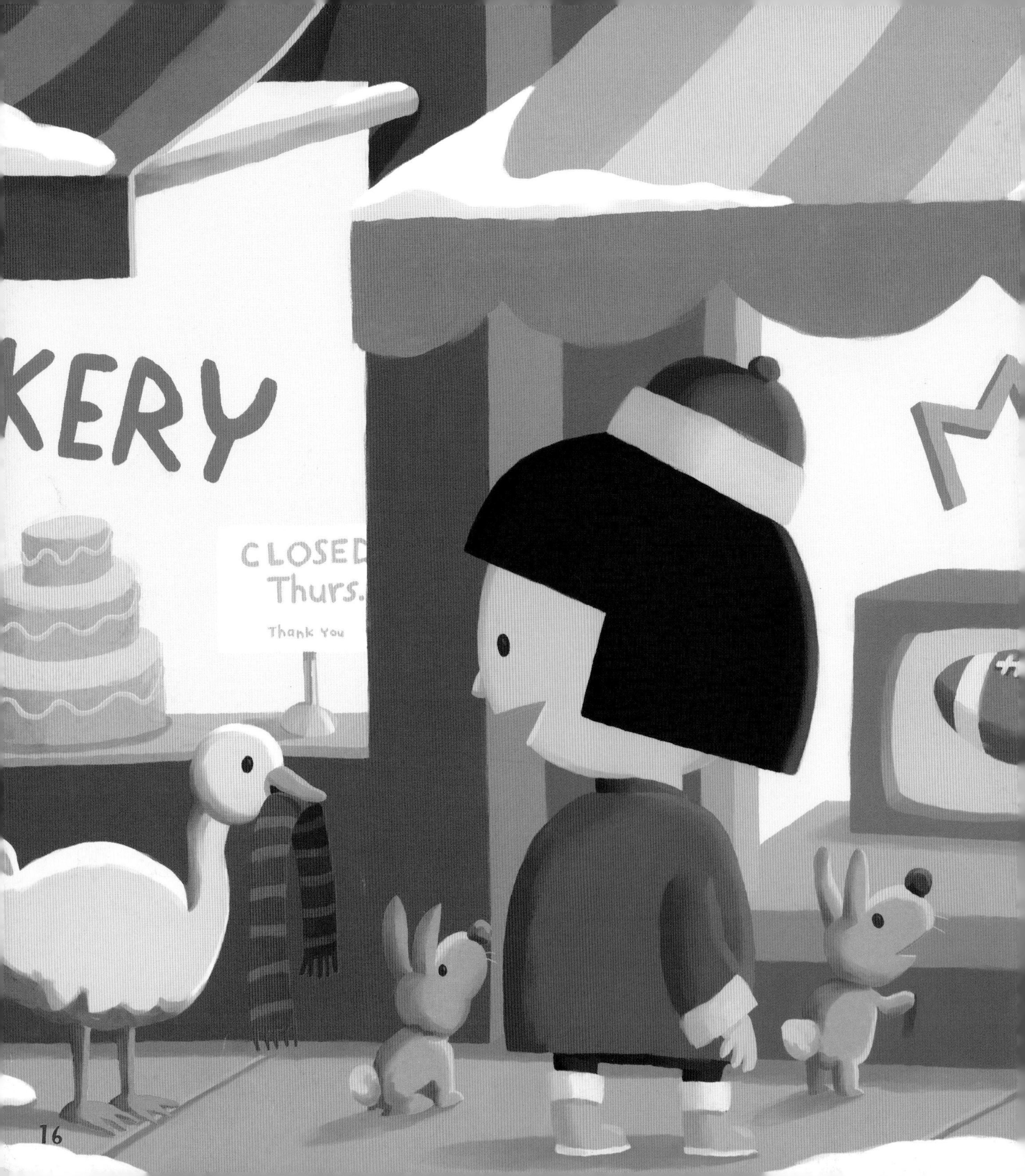
KERY
CLOSED
Thurs.
Thank You

Thank you, duck.

17

Thank you, general store.

Thank you, snow people.

Thank you, hill.

Thank you, thank you.

Thank you,
mixer.

27

Thank you, pie
with whipped cream.

Thank you,
Thanksgiving.